Three Days with

Jim

T0657802

A Red Fox Book

Published by Random House Children's Books
20 Vauxhall Bridge Road, London SW1V 2SA

A division of The Random House Group Ltd
London Melbourne Sydney Auckland
Johannesburg and agencies throughout the world

Text © Kaye Umansky 2001
Illustrations © Judy Brown 2001

3 5 7 9 10 8 6 4 2

Printed and bound in Great Britain
by Bookmarque Ltd, Croydon, Surrey

Papers used by The Random House Group Limited are natural,
recyclable products made from wood grown in sustainable forest.
The manufacturing processes conform to the environmental
regulations of the country of origin.

THE RANDOM HOUSE GROUP Limited Reg. No. 954009

www.randomhouse.co.uk

ISBN 0 09 941708 1

Three Days with Jim

Jim

Kaye Umansky

illustrated by Judy Brown

RED FOX

Jim at the Fair

Jim sat on the rug, tickling his baby sister. Her name was Jane. She smiled her gummy smile and kicked her legs.

'Jenny, Jim and Jane,' said Jim's big sister, Jenny. 'The Three Jays. We can be a pop group.'

'No way,' said Jim. 'I'm going to be a fire fighter.'

It was true. He had the helmet and everything. He slept in it sometimes.

'Dooby dooby doo!' sang Jenny, dancing around. 'Ladies and gentlemen, The Three Jays. Give them a big clap!'

'Eeee-awww eeee-awww,' went Jim, like a siren.

He zoomed around the room and frightened Moppet the cat.

He screeched to a halt, jumped out and sprayed Jane with his pretend hose.

Jane grinned and tried to eat her own foot.

'There's a fair on the common,' said Jenny. 'Mum says I can take you. But you've got to hold my hand.'

'Yipee!' yelled Jim.

'I've got five pounds,' said Jenny. 'I've been saving.'

'I haven't,' said Jim. 'I spent all my money on this helmet.'

'I'll lend you some,' said Jenny. 'But you have to pay it back.'

'I will!' promised Jim. 'I will I will I will!' He *really* wanted to go to the fair.

Jane just lay there. She didn't even know what a fair was.

The fair was big and noisy and wonderful! The air smelt of sugar and onions. There were stalls selling hot dogs, doughnuts, ice cream and bars of coconut ice. Jenny bought candyfloss, toffee apples and two fizzy drinks.

They wandered around with their mouths full, staring at everything.

There was a hoopla, a firing range and a dart throwing game, where you could win a big green gorilla.

'I don't like him,' said Jenny 'He's got a cross face. And gorillas aren't green.'

'You've got a pink frog at home,' said Jim. 'You like him.'

Jenny was right, though. The gorilla did look cross. A lot of stalls had cross green gorillas as prizes, he noticed.

But that didn't stop the fair being great.

There were pirate swings and spinning aeroplanes and a big wheel. There were dodgem cars. There was a roundabout with horses and motorbikes and, best of all, a fire engine!

Jim pointed. 'I want to go on that,' he said. 'Lucky I'm wearing my helmet.'

'In a minute,' said Jenny. 'Let's try hook the duck. That looks easy.' She pointed to a stall where wooden ducks bobbed about on water. You had to catch them by their necks with a wire hoop.

'Oh, please can I go on the roundabout?' begged Jim. He gave a little jump. 'Please? *Please?*'

'Yes. I said you can. When it stops. But first, we're hooking ducks. If you hook three in one minute, you get a prize, look. Come on, I'll let you have a go.'

'All right,' said Jim.

Jenny was right. Hook the duck *was* easy. Between them, they hooked nine.

'That's a record,' said the stall holder. 'You get a choice of the best prize. What do you want? A green gorilla or a goldfish?'

'A goldfish,' said Jenny and Jim together.

The man held out a water-filled plastic bag with a glint of orange. They both reached up at the same time.

'Who's having it, then?' said the man.

Jenny and Jim looked at each other. It had been Jenny's money that paid for it, of course, and she had hooked the most ducks.

But this was a real live goldfish! Jim wanted it so much he thought he would burst.

'We'll share,' said Jenny, kindly. 'And it can live in your room because Moppet sleeps on my bed. But I get to feed it sometimes and change the water.'

'Great,' said Jim. 'Thanks!'

Hooray! It was going to live in his room!

He took the
bag, held it up
close to his eyes
and stared hard.

The goldfish
stared back
and blew a
bubble. It
had beady
black eyes and
a fancy, frilly tail.

'What shall we call it?' asked
Jenny.

'Norman,' said Jim. 'It looks like
Mr Norman next door.'

'Don't be daft. How can a fish
look like Mr Norman next door?'

'They're both orange,' said Jim.

'Mr Norman isn't orange,' said

Jenny. 'He's got ginger hair.
Anyway, I think she's a girl fish.
Let's call her Miranda. Miranda's
a beautiful name.'

'Norman doesn't think so,' said
Jim. 'Can I go on the roundabout
now? PLEASE?'

'Go on, then,' said Jenny.
'I'll hold Miranda.'

Jim ran off at the double
before someone else could
get the fire engine.

After Jim had finished on
the roundabout, they both
had a go on the dodgems.
Jim carefully held his new pet
on his lap while Jenny drove.

It was great fun. They did
loads of crashing.

'I hope Norman isn't feeling

sea sick,' said Jim, holding up
the bag.

'I'm sure Miranda is fine,'
said Jenny, happily bashing the
car in front.

g wheel
d, but
enny
pointed out
their own
house in the
distance. Jim
wouldn't
look. He was
glad when
it was over.

Five pounds
doesn't last long
when there are two of you.
Soon, there was only twenty pence
left. They spent that on sweets.
Jim ate most of them.

'We'd better go home,' said
Jenny. 'Mum said only an hour.
And I'm hungry.'

'I'm not,' said Jim. He felt a
bit sick.

'Too many sweets, that's your
trouble,' said Jenny. 'Shall I carry
the fish now?'

'It's all right,' said Jim. 'He's not
heavy. In fact, he seems to be
getting lighter…'

They both stopped. They looked
at each other. Then they looked
down at the bag in Jim's hand.

'Ooh,' squealed Jim.

'Oh no!' gasped Jenny. 'The bag's
leaking.'

Sure enough, a
thin jet of water
was spurting out.
A trail of drips
wound away
behind them.

'It's going down fast,' said Jim.
'Help! Norman!'

'Don't let's panic,' said Jenny.
'Shush a minute. Let me think.'

Jim waited while Jenny thought.

'Can we get home in time, do you
think, before all the water's gone? If
we run?' said Jenny.

'I don't think so,' said Jim.
'The hole's getting bigger.

Do something!'

'I'm thinking, I'm thinking! You
think too. I thought you were a fire
fighter.'

'There isn't a fire.'

'No, but they're trained to deal
with all sorts of emergencies.
Floods and things. Come on.
Think!'

Jim thought.
So did Jenny.
They came
up with
the idea
at exactly the same
time.

'Your helmet!'
shouted Jenny.

'My helmet!' shouted Jim.

Jenny
undid the buckle
beneath his chin and Jim took it off.

They put the plastic bag in.
The remains of the water slopped
out, taking the new goldfish
with it.

Norman/Miranda swam around
happily in the bottom of Jim's
helmet.

'What a team,' said Jenny.

'Yep,' said Jim.

They smacked hands.

Then they went home.

That night, Jim lay in bed
watching his new pet swimming
around the pudding basin. It wasn't
the best of containers,

but they
would get him
a proper bowl tomorrow. And
some weed and food and a plastic
treasure chest.

Norman. It was a good name.

All in all, thought Jim, it had
been a really good day.

Madame Zuleka

Mabel, Dot and Shirley came round to do dressing up with Jenny. They shut the bedroom door on Jim.

'You can't come in,' they said. 'Not yet.'

Jim hung around on the landing until he got bored. Then he went downstairs and opened the front door to see if it was still raining.

It was.

When he went back up to Jenny's room, the door was still closed. There was a lot of giggling going on. Someone was shaking a tambourine.

'Can I come in now?' he shouted.

'No! Go away,' they shouted. 'Come back later.'

So Jim went away again. He kicked a ball down the hall, but there was no one to kick it back. He didn't fancy colouring his poster. There was too much sky to fill in.

He sat in the big chair and picked up the book that lay open on the arm. It had pictures of dinosaurs. Jenny was reading it to him. He wondered how long her friends would stay.

When Jim went back later, there was a sign on Jenny's door. It was done in gold and silver. There were moons and stars and suns. It read:

MADAME ZULEKA
FORTUNE TELLER
KNOCK 3 TIMES

Jim knocked three times. The door opened mysteriously.

It was dark inside the room. The only light came from the bedside lamp, which was covered with green tissue paper. There were lots of scarves draped everywhere. Cut out silver stars hung from the ceiling. The floor was deep in cushions and pillows.

'Come into my tent, O child,' said a deep voice, from out of the spooky green darkness. 'I am Madame Zuleka and these are my assistants, Carleeta, Rosalinda and Pearl.'

Carleeta, Rosalinda
and Pearl wore lots
of red lipstick.
They had bangles
on their arms and
scarves on their
heads. Pearl wore a
pair of high-heeled
lady's shoes.

'Come, O child,
you may enter,'
said Carleeta,
who was Mabel.

'Yes,' said
Rosalinda,
who was Dot.
'Come.'

Pearl was
Shirley. She
just giggled.

Madame Zuleka wore a red shawl, big hoop earrings and sunglasses. She sat on a cushion with her legs crossed, waving her hands over something big and round. It was covered with a red cloth, but Jim knew what it was.

'What are you doing with Norman?' asked Jim.

'If you mean Miranda, she's my crystal ball,' said Jenny. 'You don't mind, do you? I'm not hurting her.'

'I suppose not,' said Jim.

'Sit, O child,' said Carleeta, pointing to the floor.

'No, kneel,' said Rosalinda. 'There, on that cushion.'

Shirley was taking the lady's shoes off because they hurt a bit.

'What is your name, O child?' asked Madame Zuleka, from behind her dark glasses.

'Jim,' said Jim.

'Well, cross my palm with silver, Jim, and I will look into my ball and see what I can see.'

'I haven't got any silver,' said Jim.

'Just pretend,' said Dot.

So he did.

'I shall now look deep into the crystal,' said Madame Zuleka.

Slowly, she raised the red cloth
and peered beneath. 'Soon, all
will be revealed. Assistants!
Sprinkle the Magic Dust! Let
the dance begin!'

The three assistants did a dance
and threw handfuls of glitter around.
Carleeta shook the tambourine
and Rosalinda
and Pearl

waved their arms about, making their bangles jangle.

'Deep,' muttered Madame Zuleka. 'Deeeeep...'

Jim giggled. What with the green lamp and everything, it was almost quite scary.

'YessSS!' hissed Madame Zuleka. 'The mists are clearing. I see it all!

'Oh no!' She gave a gasp. 'Assistants three! Come and see!'

Carleeta, Rosalinda and Pearl gathered round and gasped. Their eyes were very round. 'What?' said Jim.

Up to then, he had been having fun. 'What's the matter?'

'Danger!' said Madame Zuleka. 'I see danger ahead! Beware! A journey lies before you. First, you must cross over the Googy Waters to the Isle of Wild Waggoo!'

The assistants fell about laughing.

'And then,' went on Madame Zuleka, 'you will climb the high, sharp Mountains of Pingapointy, where eagles dare not walk.'

'Fly, you mean,' said Dot, and everyone giggled again.

'Last of all,' said Madame Zuleka, 'you will cross the burning Desert of Dong, where the quick sands suck you down. Then, and only then, will you get your Heart's Desire.'

'What does that mean?' asked Jim.

'It's what you want most of all. Any more questions?'

'No,' said Jim, who was feeling a bit hot.

'Assistants! Show him out.'

Carleeta opened the door and Rosalinda and Pearl pushed Jim out. When he was on the landing, he said, 'Mum says it's nearly tea time and do Mabel and Dot and Shirley want to stay and if so will jam sandwiches do?'

'Yes please,' said Mabel and Dot together.

'I can't,' said Shirley. 'My cousin's coming.'

'We'd better get changed,' said Jenny. And they shut the door.

Jim decided to go into the garden.
It had finally stopped raining and
he needed some fresh air. It had
been stuffy in Jenny's room. It had
smelled a bit of feet, too. He was
glad he didn't have to help clear

it up.
All that
glitter.

Still, it
had been
quite fun.
Jenny
made a
good
fortune
teller. He had liked the sound of the
journey with all the dangers. Of
course, none of those things could
really happen. Could they?

Everything sparkled after the
rain. There was a big puddle lying
right across the
garden path.

'Over the Googy Waters to the
Isle of Wild Waggoo,' thought Jim.
He took a running jump at
the puddle and landed safely in a
flower bed. He didn't even get his
feet wet.

He walked around the side of
the house to the back. Jim's dad
was getting a new lawn laid. There
was a big, slippery pile of muddy
rolls of turf at the end of the
garden. Jim wasn't supposed to
play around here, but he did if
no one was watching.

'Up the high, sharp Mountains
of Pingapointy,'
thought Jim,
climbing up
the pile.
'Where
eagles dare
not fly.'

He reached the top. It really was quite high and very slippery. He took a deep breath, dug his heels in and pushed off.

He skidded safely down the steep slope, keeping his balance and not falling down once.

Only the sandpit lay between him and the kitchen door.

'Here I go, over the burning Desert of Dong where the quicksands suck you down,' thought Jim,

crunching through the sand, which stuck to his muddy shoes. Taking care to avoid the quicksands, he reached the other side before he knew it.

And that was it. Quick change, hide muddy shoes, then tea. He was looking forward to tea. He loved jam sandwiches. Strawberry was his favourite.

After tea, he would go and spend some time with Norman. He made a good crystal ball, but a much better fish. It was the same with Jenny. Madame Zuleka was all right, but Jenny was better.

Maybe she would read him some
more of the dinosaur book when
her friends went home.

And later, that was just what
he got.

Jim in the Snow

One night, the best thing
happened. It snowed.
    Jim didn't
know at
first,

because the curtains
were drawn. He yawned and
stretched and looked at his watch.

It was a fire fighter's
watch. It was big.
It was new.
You pressed
buttons and
a red light
flashed and it
made a noise like
a siren. Jim loved it.

'Morning, Norman,' said Jim to
his goldfish. Everything seemed
quieter than usual. The light was
funny. He padded to the window
and drew back the curtain.

'Yeeeeeeeessssss!' yelled
Jim.

The garden was white and clean
and perfect, except for a trail of
Moppet's paw prints on the lawn.
The window ledge was piled high.

Jim opened the window and grabbed a fistful of snow.

Ouch! It was so cold it hurt.

He ran into Jenny's room and put his freezing hand on the back of her neck.

'Ahhh!' screamed Jenny. 'Get off!'

'It's snowed!' shouted Jim.

'Wheeee!' went Jenny, throwing off her duvet and bouncing up and down on the bed.

Washing and teeth took one minute.

Dressing took two minutes.

Then it was coats, boots and out the door into the weird white world!

They made snow people first. They made a Jenny snowgirl and

decorated her with scarves and the big red shawl from Jenny's dressing-up box.

They made a Jim snowboy, with an onion nose. Jim went and got his

fire fighter's helmet.
It looked good on
the snowboy.

Baby Jane was
too little to go
outside in the
snow. She sat in
her high chair,
messing about
with her food
and watching them
through the window.

'We'd better make a snowbaby
too,' said Jenny. 'She'll feel left out,
poor thing.'

'I'm glad I'm not a baby any
more,' said Jim. 'Playing in the
snow's better than sitting around
with your dinner on your head.'

They both giggled.

They made a snowbaby and
dressed her in a bonnet and one of
Jane's bibs. They tucked a bottle
under one snowy arm. Jane grinned
out the window and banged her
beaker on the window pane.

'I think she likes it,' said Jim.

Making three snow people was
tiring. They lay on their backs
and made snow angels, which was
quite restful.

Soon, a crowd of children came
along the street. There was Sam,
Jilly, Kate, Bess, Brad, Gail, Mabel
and Bruce.

They had tin trays.

'We're going sledging in the park!' they shouted. 'We've got trays!'

'Wait for us!' shouted Jenny and Jim. 'We're coming, too!' And they ran indoors to find a tray.

It was huge fun in the park. Everything looked quite different under the thick blanket of snow. It lined the branches of the trees and lay thickly on the still swings.

A snowball fight broke out.
Mike, Dave and George, the big boys, came along and joined in. It was great fun until Bess got a snowball in her face and cried a bit and all the girls stopped in support. Then they walked on to the sloping bit of the park and took turns sliding down the hill on the trays. That was wonderful. Even Bess cheered up.

Finally it began to snow again, and everyone was freezing and hungry, so they all went home except for Mike, Dave and George, who went to the chip shop.

It wasn't until he got home that Jim discovered that his watch was missing!

'It's gone!' said Jim, staring down at his empty wrist.

They were in the hall.

'What has?' said Jenny, pulling off cold, wet socks.

'My fire fighter watch,' said Jim.

'It can't have,' said Jenny. 'It'll be up your sleeve or something.'

But it wasn't.

'Can we go back?' begged Jim. 'Can we go back and look for it?'

'No point,' said Jenny. 'It's snowing again. If you dropped it, it'll be covered up by now. Do you want fish fingers or soup?'

'Fish fingers,' said Jim. But he didn't really care. He wasn't hungry. He had lost his watch and everything was spoilt.

After lunch, Shirley and Clare came calling for Jenny. Clare had her grandad's proper wooden toboggan.

Her dad was going to take them to a real hill, out in the country. They had a big flask of soup.

'There's only room for three in the car,' said Clare, looking at Jim.

'I don't want to go anyway,' said Jim. 'I'm a bit tired.'

Off went the girls into the crisp, clean snow.

Jim cried a bit. He just couldn't help it. Then he went to his room and sat quietly with Norman, trying to think hopeful thoughts. Perhaps  Jenny would find it in the street. She might come running in waving it in her hand. It was possible.

But she didn't.

That night, in bed, Jim cried a lot.

Next day, the sun came out and the snow began to melt. Everything looked grubby again. Jim's friend Bruce came round to ask if Jim could play.

'He's still in bed,' said Jenny. 'He says he's got a tummy ache.'

So Bruce went away.

Upstairs, Jim lay and stared at the ceiling. He didn't have a tummy ache. He had a lost watch ache. It really hurt.

'The snow's nearly gone, worst luck,' said Jenny, poking her head round the door. 'Mum says do you want eggy soldiers?'

'No thanks,' said Jim, with a sigh.

Some days are just awful, he thought. No snow. No watch. It was all too much.

'Shall I do a puzzle with you?'
'Not right now, thanks,' said Jim.
'Want to colour in?'
'I think I'll just lie for a bit,' said Jim. 'Thanks.'

'All right,' said Jenny. 'I'm going to the park. I'm meeting the others. See you later.'

'See you,' said Jim.

'Where's Jim?' asked Shirley as Jenny came running up.

'Home,' said Jenny. 'He's still upset about his watch. I'd better look for it, now the snow's thawed.'

'We'll help,' said Clare, Dot and Mabel.

They hunted high and low. Some other children came and joined in the search. They looked for a long time, but there was no sign of the watch. Finally, they all got bored and made a den instead.

When Jenny got home, Jim was watching television in the big chair, with Moppet on his lap.

'Any luck?' said Jim.

'No,' said Jenny. 'Sorry. We did try. What are you watching?'

'Nothing much.'

The rest of the day dragged slowly by. Jim was glad when it was bedtime again.

There was a moon that night, peeping from behind a lot of big, black clouds. Three dirty, lumpy, rather sad-looking snow people stood in Jim's garden. They were all that was left of the snow.

The cat flap clattered, and out jumped Moppet, in a kittenish mood. She saw the snow people and ran over to investigate.

She put out a paw and patted the snowboy's onion nose. The onion rolled into the fire fighter's helmet, which lay on its side. Moppet pounced, all four paws landing at the same time.

Suddenly, from beneath the helmet, there came... a red flashing light and the noise of a siren!

Moppet leapt away, fur on end, and backed towards the fence.

There was a little pause. Then came the sound of a window opening upstairs, followed by the loudest, happiest yell you ever have heard.

'Whoopeeeeeeeeee!' yelled Jim.

Grinning from ear to ear, he stared down at the small red, flashing light where his watch lay wailing for him to come on down and get it.

Jenny's window shot open. From inside came another happy whoop. They leaned out over their windowsills and grinned at each other.

From downstairs came the sound of Baby Jane's happy gurgle.

And just then, to make everything simply perfect, it started to snow again.

FOX TALES

THREE LINKED STORIES, IDEAL FOR BUILDING READING CONFIDENCE.

Bottomley at Large
Peter Harris & Doffy Weir

The Megamogs in Moggymania
Peter Haswell

Totally Trevor!
Rob Lewis

Three Days with Jim
Kaye Umansky & Judy Brown

FOX TALES

AVAILABLE NOW!